Sit Tog!

Written by Fiona Undrill

Illustrated by Sylwia Filipczak

Collins

Tig sits. Tag naps.

Tog taps the top.

Sit Tog. Tog sit!

Tig nags. Tag nods.

Tog taps. Tog pats.

It sags. It tips.

Sit Tog. Tog sit!

Mad Tig tips in.

Tog dips the mop.

Sad Tag tips in.

Tag pats. Tig taps.

Tog dips in!

pop

/g/

14

 After reading

Letters and Sounds: Phase 2

Word count: 48

Focus phonemes: /g/ /o/

Common exception word: the

Curriculum links: Personal, social and emotional development

Early learning goals: Reading: read and understand simple sentences; use phonic knowledge to decode regular words and read them aloud accurately; read some irregular words

Developing fluency

- Your child may enjoy hearing you read the book.
- Take turns to read a page. Encourage your child to read with expression, using a bossy tone for the sentences that end in an exclamation mark on pages 4 and 8.

Phonic practice

- On pages 4–5, ask your child to find and sound out the word **Tog**. (t/o/g – **Tog**) Next, ask them to find the word **nods**. Point out the same /o/ sound in the middle of these words.
- On pages 10–11, ask them to find the words that have the /i/ sound. (*dips, tips, in*)
- Look at the "I spy sounds" pages (14–15). Point to the gate on page 15 and say: I spy a /g/ in gate. Challenge your child to point to and name different things they can see containing a /g/ sound. Help them to identify /g/, asking them to repeat the word and listen out for the /g/ sound. Point out that the /g/ is not always at the beginning of the word. (e.g. *Tig, Tog, Tag, grass, grapes, grin, glasses, glass (drinking glass), grasshopper, bug, frog*)

Extending vocabulary

- Turn to page 9. Ask your child: Can you think of a different word you could use instead of **tips**? (e.g. *falls, tumbles*)